Palanquin

7 OF 12

POLANQEE

OPHELIA HOUSE
SHADOW OF THE HIVE

OPHELIA HOUSE
SHADOW OF THE HIVE

ORIGINAL ARTWORK

ANDREW L. WILLIS

CREATED AND WRITTEN

CARLTON L. SAMPSON

COVER DESIGN, BALLOONS, PAGE LAYOUT

Palanquin

THE OPHEDIAN QANAT

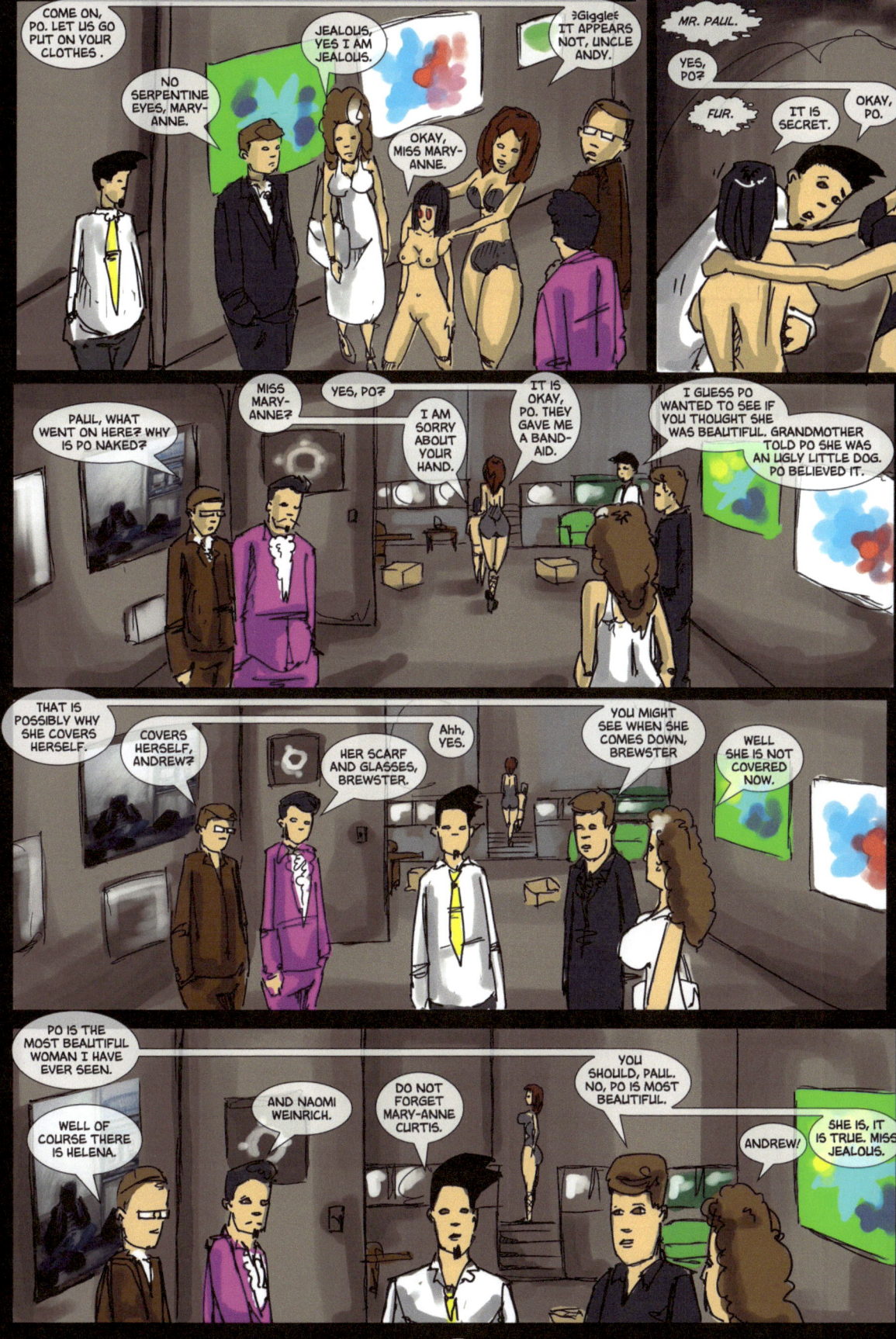

- 7 -

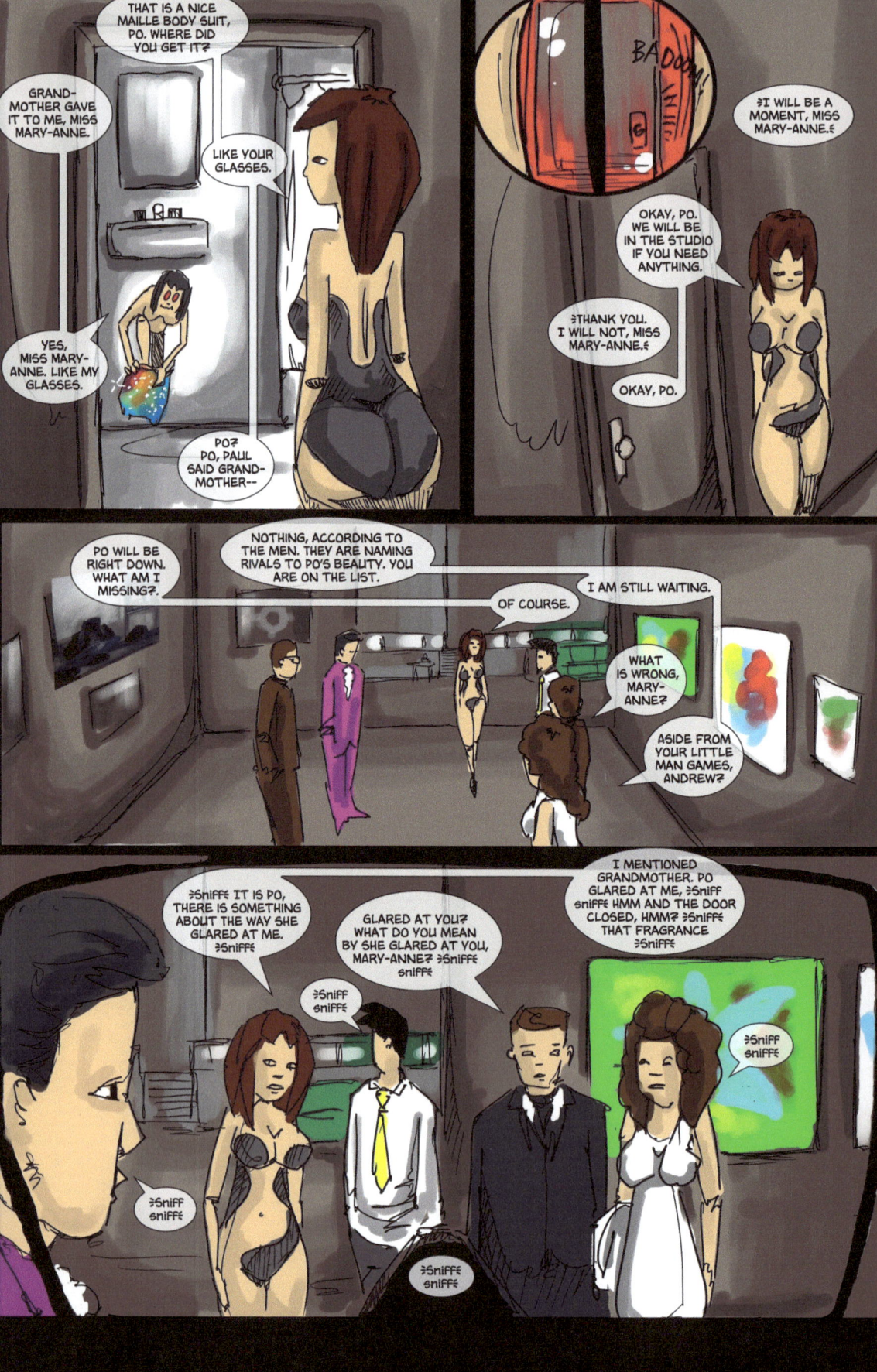

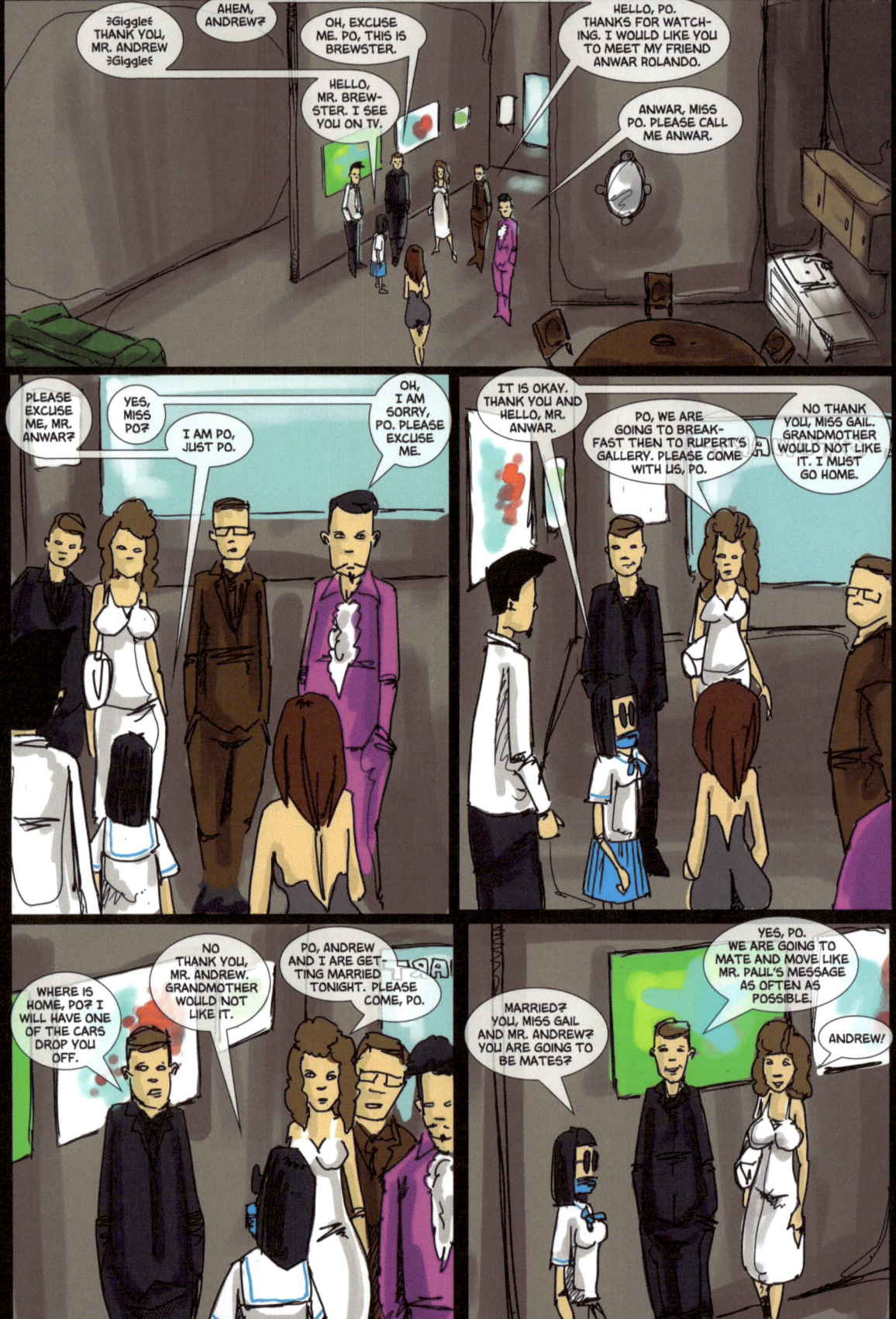

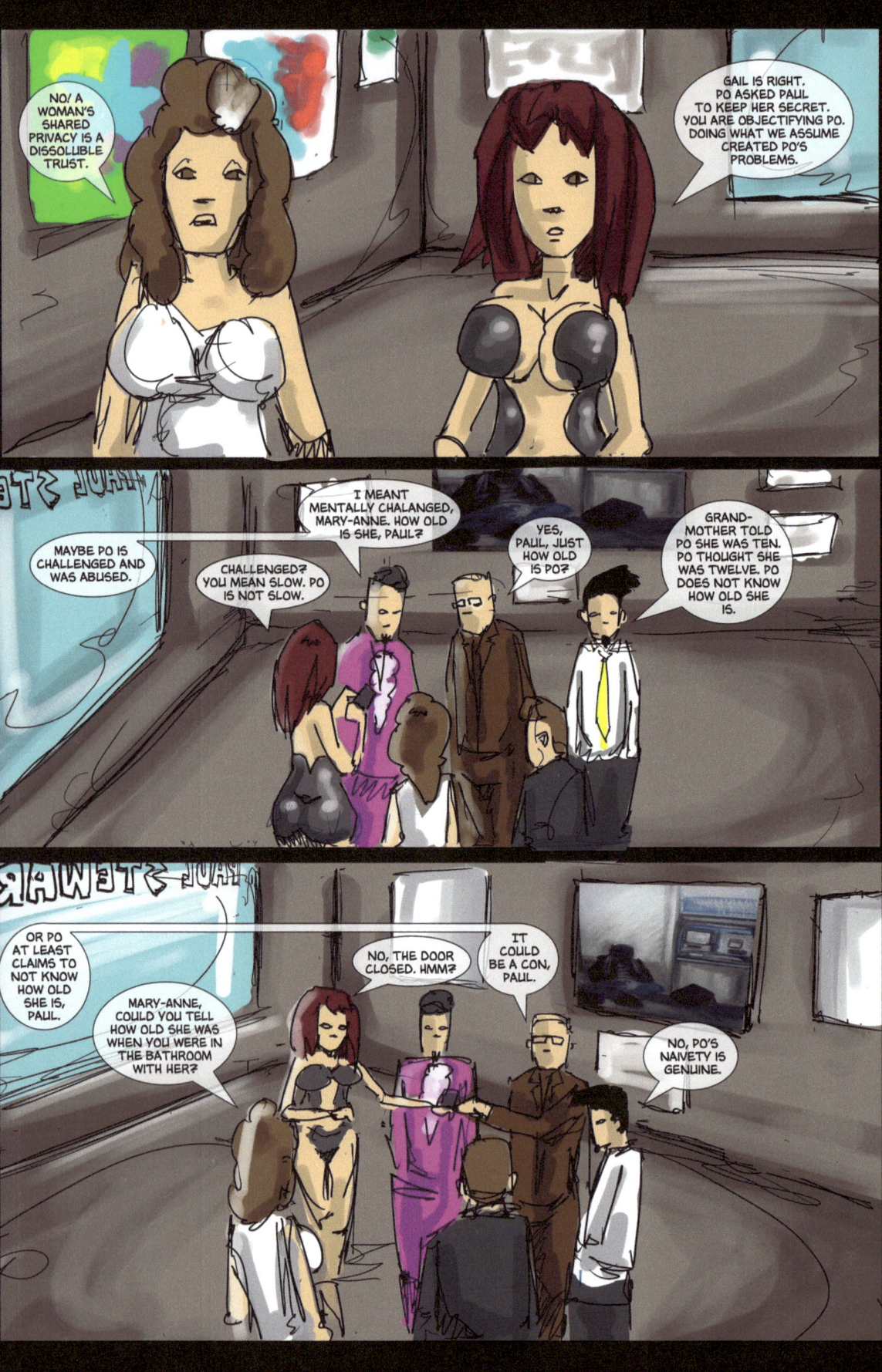

SIRYN SISTERS WILL PUT ME BACK ON MY LEASH;

PUT ME BACK IN MY CAGE.

GRANDMOTHER SEE ME AND MR.--

OH.

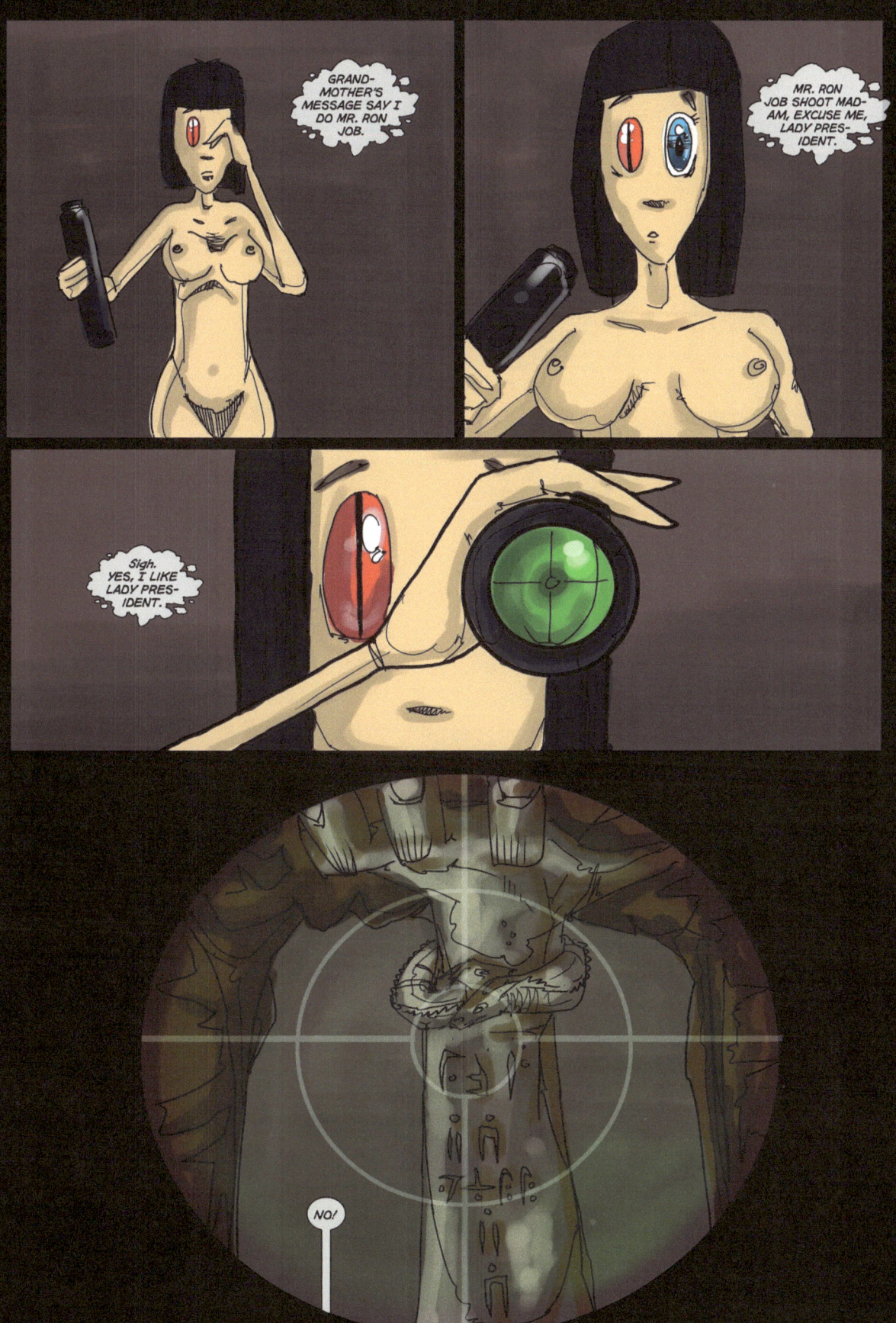

GRAND-MOTHER'S MESSAGE SAY...
...TAKE MR. RON HANDS...
...MAKE GLOVES.

GLOVES LIKE CLOTHES, BUT JUST FOR HANDS.

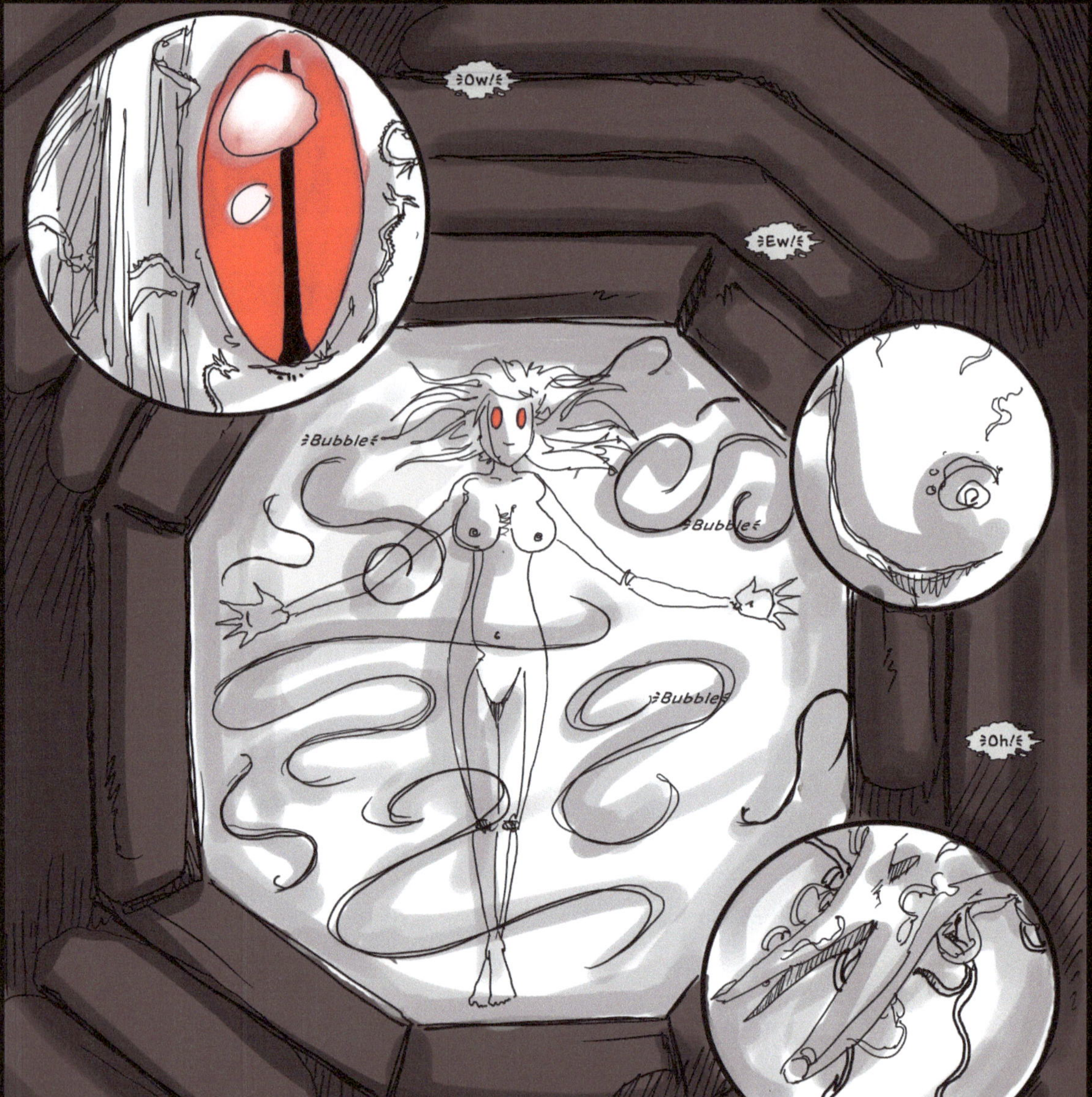

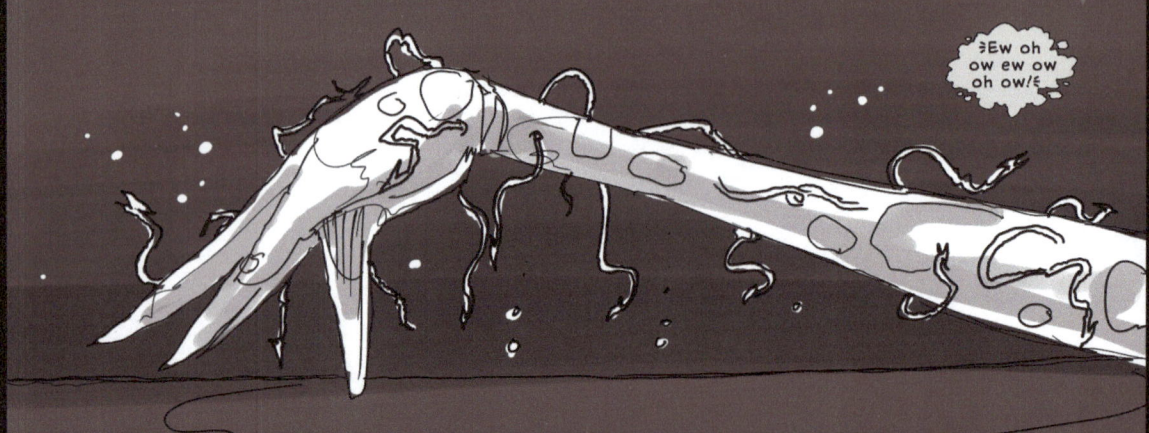

WHY YOU WAIT HERE?
OH, Giggle giggle. OKAY I TELL YOU. Giggle.
FIRST TIME I LET MR. PAUL SEE ME. I WEAR MY COAT.
I ASK MR. PAUL FOR DATE.
MR. PAUL SAY NO.
I THINK I AM UGLY LITTLE DOG.
BUT LATER, MR. PAUL SEE ME IN HIS LAIR WITHOUT MY COAT.
Giggle giggle. MR. PAUL SAY I MOST BEAUTIFUL WO-MAN HE EVER SEE. Giggle.
Sigh. YES HUMANS SAY IT IMPROPER FOR ME AND MR. PAUL TO BE ALONE IN HIS LAIR.
BUT I NOT HUMAN. Giggle.
AND MR. PAUL'S MOVING MESSAGE SAY TO STALK MR. PAUL.
SO I GO TO MR. PAUL'S LAIR.

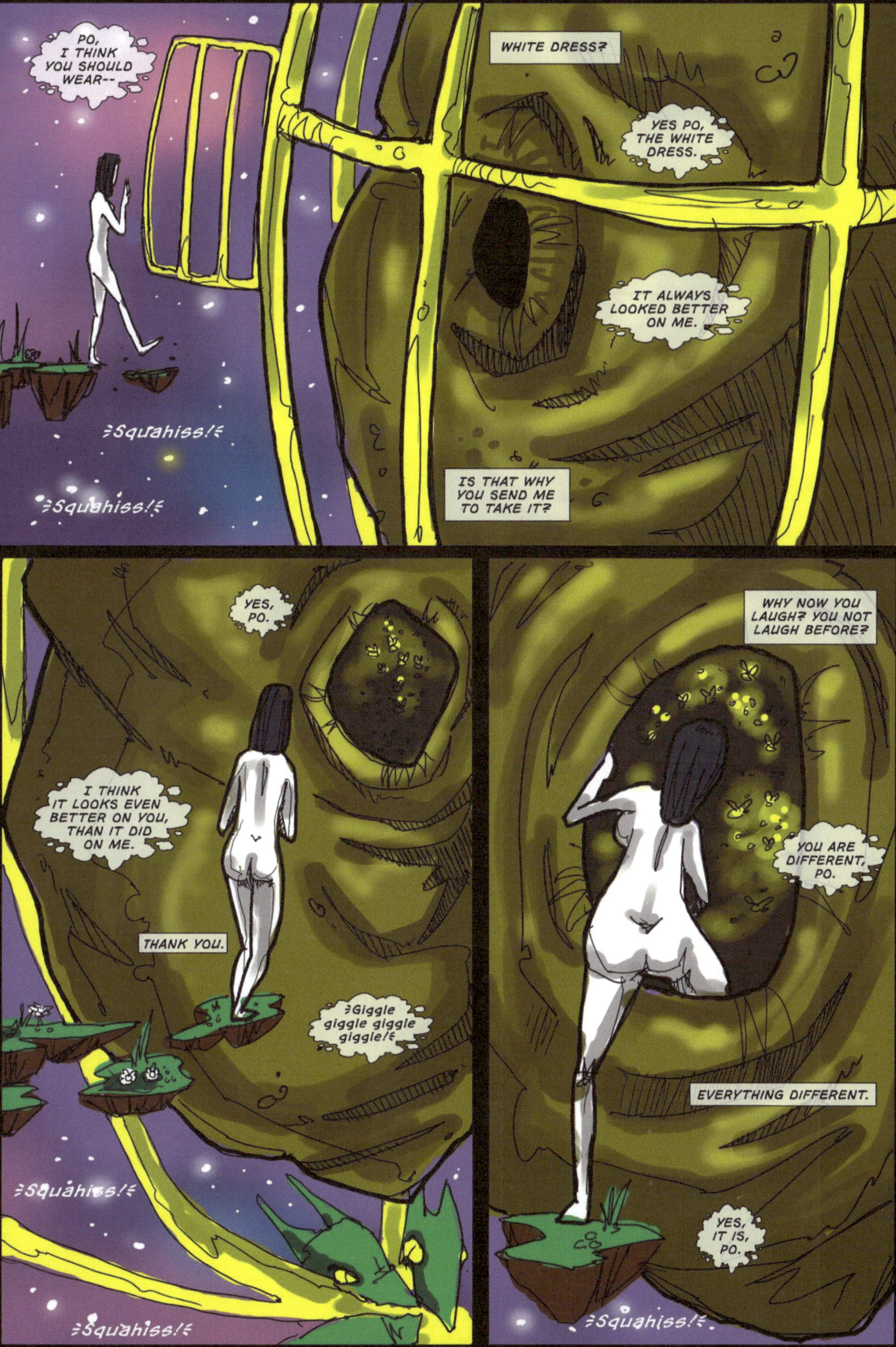
PO, I THINK YOU SHOULD WEAR--
WHITE DRESS?
YES PO, THE WHITE DRESS.
IT ALWAYS LOOKED BETTER ON ME.
IS THAT WHY YOU SEND ME TO TAKE IT?
Squahiss!
Squahiss!
YES, PO.
I THINK IT LOOKS EVEN BETTER ON YOU, THAN IT DID ON ME.
THANK YOU.
Giggle giggle giggle giggle!
Squahiss!
Squahiss!
WHY NOW YOU LAUGH? YOU NOT LAUGH BEFORE?
YOU ARE DIFFERENT, PO.
EVERYTHING DIFFERENT.
YES, IT IS, PO.
Squahiss!

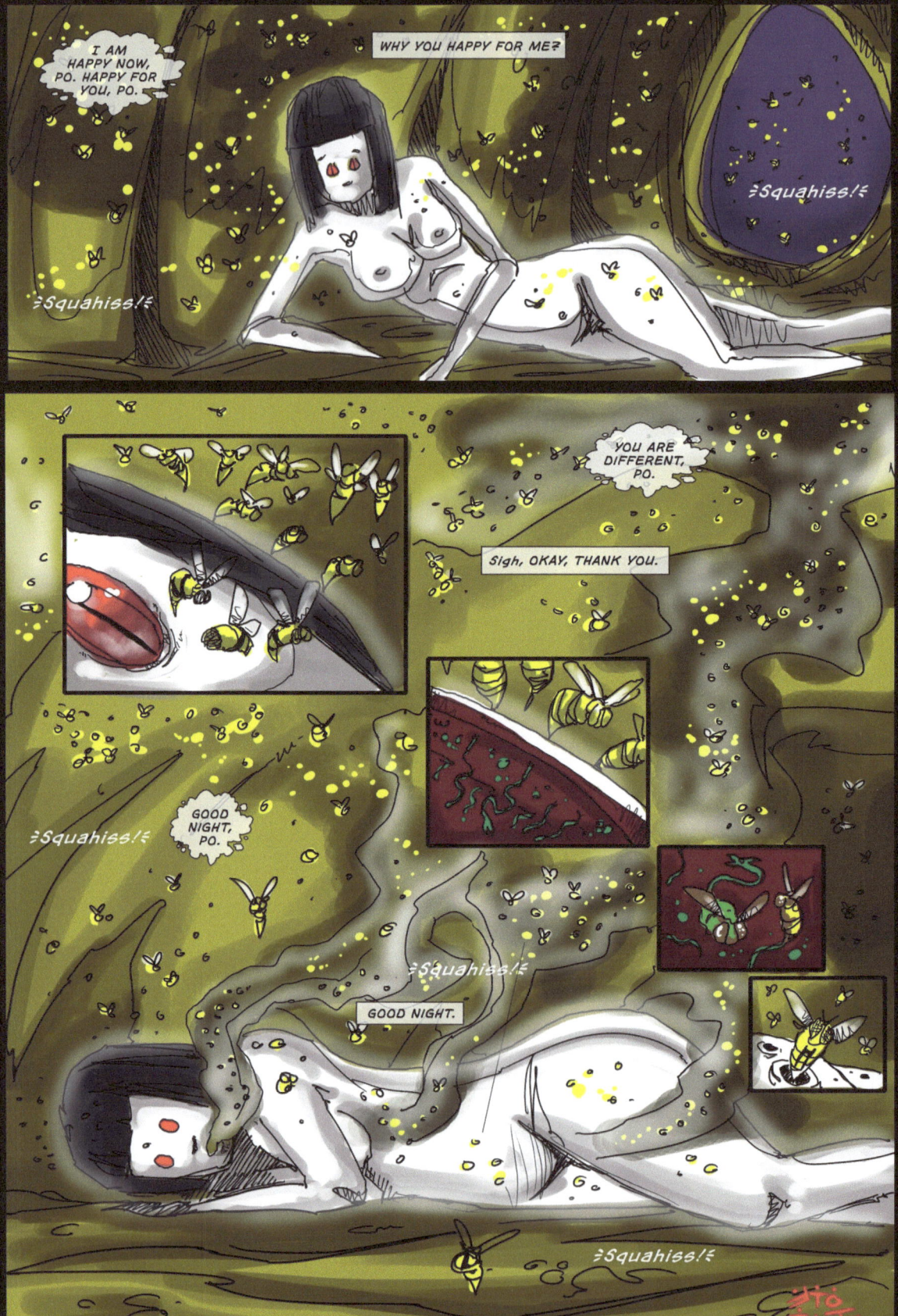

PO LYN LEE
OPHELIA HOUSE
NEXT ISSUE

"LUNCH AT LANGLEY'S"

IT IS BARBARA LANGLEY'S AFTERNOON MIXER.
MUCH TO WILLIAM RANDOLPH CURTIS THE
FIFTH'S SURPRISE, AN E.A.I.C. OPERATIVE TELLS
LIZ HOW THE CRIMSON LOTUS TIES TO THE
CURTIS FAMILY, MOTHER PI LYN, AND SWEET
OLD JO. TRUTH IS ON THE MENU, BUT MUM
FINDS MI QUO'S ORDER HARD TO READ. IT IS
SMOOTH SAILING AND A BURNING DESIRE FOR
PO'S DREAMBOAT MR. PAUL WHEN ALI KAHN
DOES WHAT IS RIGHT FOR THE TA SHEN LING.

CARLTON L. SAMPSON

POET, GRAPHIC NOVELL AUTHOR
CARLTON@POLYNLEE.COM
OTHER WORK AVAILABLE AT:
WWW.PHASCISTCLOWNS.COM

ANDREW L. WILLIS

AKA, THIOBIS THE ARTIST
FINE ART, SCULPTURE, ANIMATION,
MUSIC, AND WRITTEN.
ANDREW@POLYNLEE.COM
OTHER WORK AVAILABLE AT:
WWW.WAOOBAKEARTWORK.COM

COPY EDITOR "THE MUSE"

THE SAYLORE PALACE HOTEL

IT IS BARBARA LANGLEY'S AFTERNOON MIXER. MUCH TO WILLIAM
RANDOLPH CURTIS THE FIFTH'S SURPRISE, AN E.A.I.C. OPERATIVE TELLS LIZ HOW
THE CRIMSON LOTUS TIES TO THE CURTIS FAMILY, MOTHER PI LYN, AND SWEET
OLD JO. TRUTH IS ON THE MENU, BUT MUM FINDS MI QUO'S ORDER HARD TO
READ. IT IS SMOOTH SAILING AND A BURNING DESIRE FOR PO'S DREAMBOAT
MR. PAUL WHEN ALI KAHN DOES WHAT IS RIGHT FOR THE TA SHEN LING.

NEXT ISSUE

WWW.POLYNLEE.COM

www.ingramcontent.com/pod-product-compliance
Lightning Source LLC
Chambersburg PA
CBHW041539240626

47164CB00002B/57